Katie Loves the Kittens

John Himmelman

Henry Holt and Company ♥ New York

For Katie, who loved the kittens
—J. H.

Henry Holt and Company, LLC
PUBLISHERS SINCE 1866
175 Fifth Avenue
New York, New York 10010
www.HenryHoltKids.com

Distributed in Canada by H. B. Fenn and Company Ltd.

Library of Congress Cataloging-in-Publication Data
Himmelman, John.
Katie loves the kittens / John Himmelman.—1st ed.
p.   cm.
Summary: When Sara Ann brings home three little kittens, Katie the dog's
enthusiasm frightens the kittens away, until she learns that quiet patience
is sometimes needed to begin a friendship.
[1. Dogs—Fiction. 2. Cats—Fiction. 3. Animals—Infancy—Fiction.
4. Patience—Fiction. 5. Friendship—Fiction.] I. Title.
PZ7.H5686Kat 2008   [E]—dc22   2007040896

ISBN-13: 978-0-8050-8682-9 / ISBN-10: 0-8050-8682-X
First Edition—2008 / Designed by Véronique Lefèvre Sweet
The artist used black Prismacolor pencils and watercolors
to create the illustrations for this book.
Printed in the United States of America on acid-free paper. ∞

1 3 5 7 9 10 8 6 4 2

Today was the most exciting day in Katie's whole life! Sara Ann had brought home three little ~~kittens~~

Katie loved those kittens so much. As soon as she saw them, she howled "AROOOOOO! AROOOOOO!" She always howled like that when she was very happy.

But Katie's howling frightened the kittens.
They ran in all directions. Katie chased them
around the house. "AROOOOO! AROOOOO!"
she howled.

"No, no, no, Katie," said Sara Ann. "You are scaring the kittens! You stay away from them until they get used to you."

Katie felt sad. She did not want to scare
the kittens.

Later that day, Sara Ann was playing with her new pets. Katie watched from around a corner. She wanted to play with the kittens too. She just loved them so much.

She tried to
control herself.

She tried and
tried and tried.

But Katie couldn't stop herself any longer.

She burst into the room. The kittens scattered.

"AROOOOO! AROOOOO!" she howled as she chased them around the room.

"No, Katie, no!" said Sara Ann. "You scared them again!"

Katie felt even sadder than before.
Poor little kittens, she thought.

That night the kittens slept with Sara Ann
in her bed. Katie missed them already.

Katie went out the kitchen door.

She looked up at Sara Ann's window.
That's where the kittens are, she thought.

She climbed up the bushes and looked in the window. The kittens were fast asleep.

Oh, what sweet little kittens, she thought.
I would love to smell them. She sniffed as hard
as she could, but they were too far away.

She quietly
climbed onto
the windowsill.

She quietly
slid under the
window. . . .

And leapt on the bed! The kittens went flying in the air. Katie was so excited. "AROOOOO! AROOOOO!" she howled.

Sara Ann picked up the dog. "Katie, what am I going to do with you? Don't you like these kittens?"

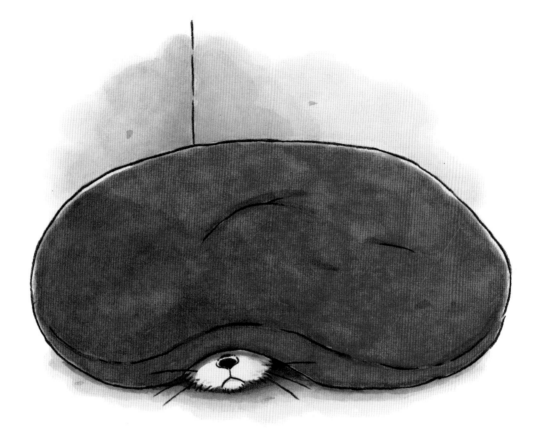

Katie felt very, very sad.

In the morning, Katie walked into the kitchen.

Three bowls of food waited for her.

She ate
the first bowl.
Mmmm, this is
good, she thought.

She ate the
second bowl.

Yummyummyummyum, she thought.

When she was halfway through the last bowl, Sara Ann walked in.

"Oh, Katie! You ate the kittens' food," she said.

Oh no, thought Katie. Now she felt sadder than ever. She went to her bed and lay down. I love those little kittens so much, she thought, and all I do is scare them and eat their food.

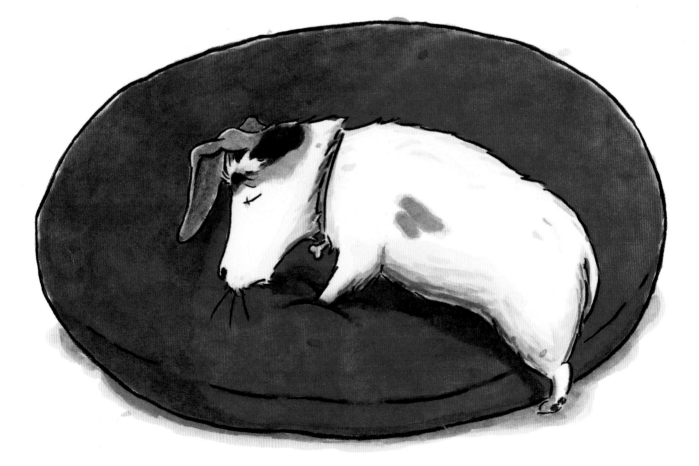

Katie stayed in her bed all day. After a while, she fell asleep.

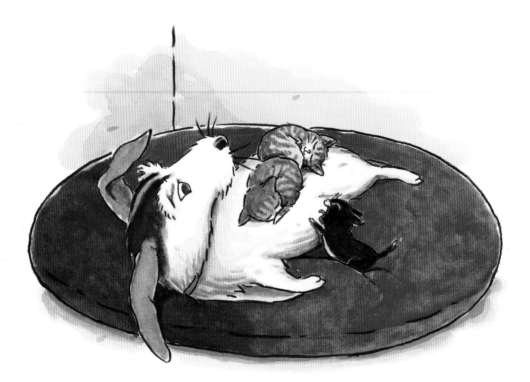

When she woke up, she was not alone.
The kittens had fallen asleep on top of her!

Katie was so happy she wanted to howl.
She wanted to jump!

She wanted to chase them all over the
room and run around in circles and play
with them!

But she didn't.

"That's my good little Katie," said Sara Ann.